That's My Job!

By Jacquese Groves

Illustrated By Annastasia Arnold

ChocolateBlue Publishing
Nashville, TN 37203

Chocolate

Publisher: Jacquese Groves, ChocolateBlue, LLC
Illustrator: Annastasia Arnold
Editor: John Fox, Bookfox

Printed in the United States of America
First Edition: October 2021

ISBN Paperback: 978-1-7358993-1-2

Library of Congress Control Number: 2021917375

For Rasheed
#hustlestrong

Myles and Malcom were best friends
who were more like brothers.
Everybody called them M&M.

Today they were in class waiting on their teacher Mr. Rasheed to make the morning announcements. On Mondays, Mr. Rasheed assigned the class helper jobs. Myles had been anxiously awaiting his turn to be the hall monitor because the hall monitor got to wear an official vest. Malcom was so chill he didn't care what job he got.

"WHAT?!" Myles whispered angrily
"I don't want to be the line leader
I wanted hall monitor.
Malcom stole my job!"

Myles walked around with an attitude all day. He was a terrible line leader! When it was time to go to lunch, he led his class right past the cafeteria.

When it was time to go to the restroom, he led everyone to the playground.

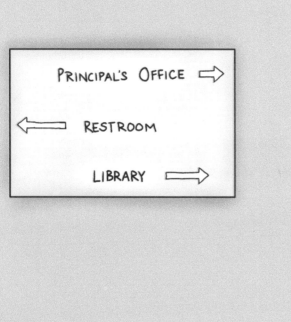

PRINCIPAL'S OFFICE ⇨

⇦ RESTROOM

LIBRARY ⇨

EXIT

When it was time to go to the playground, he led them to the library.
To make matters worse, every time Myles went the wrong way,
Malcom had to correct him because HE was the hall monitor.
Myles couldn't wait for this day to be over!

At the end of the day, when the boys were getting their backpacks from their cubbies, Malcom asked Myles what was up with him.

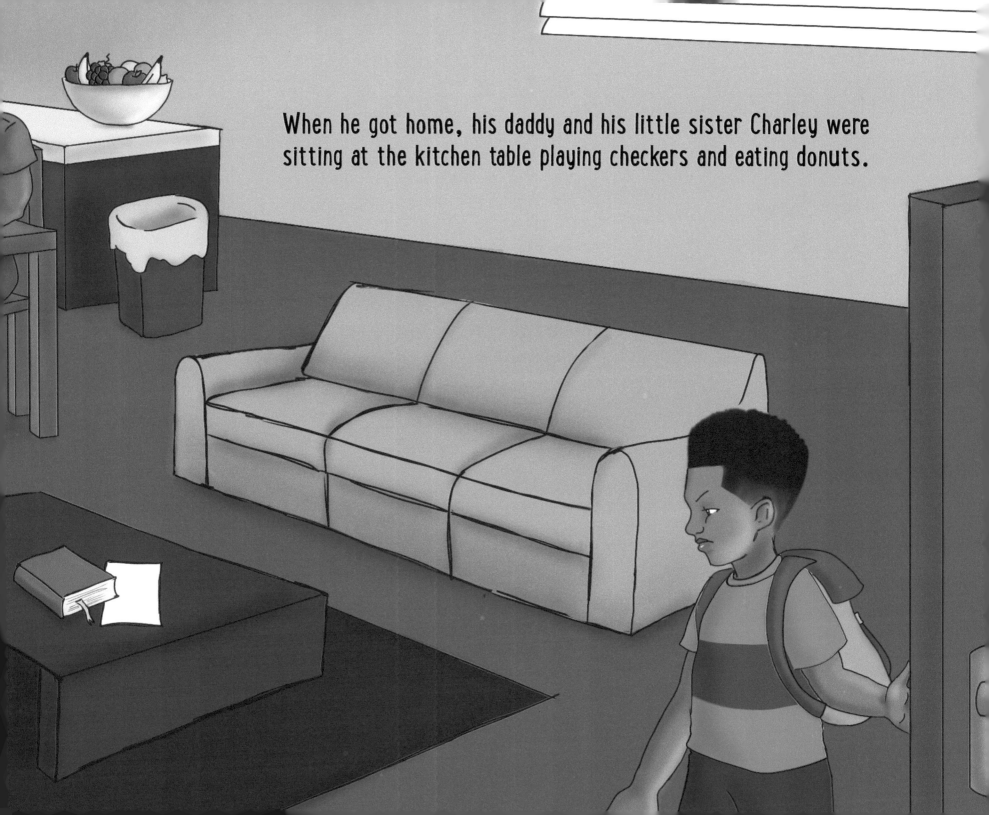

When he got home, his daddy and his little sister Charley were sitting at the kitchen table playing checkers and eating donuts.

Myles wanted a donut too.

His daddy wanted to know why he was inside the house instead of in his clubhouse with Malcom.

Myles fussed that Mr. Rasheed had made Malcom the hall monitor and him the line leader even though he wanted to be the hall monitor so he was mad at Malcom for stealing his job.

"I see," his daddy said. "Hey baby girl, why don't you take that last donut." Charley smiled and took a big bite.

"Hey, I wanted that last donut!" Myles grumbled.

"I know. Now are you mad at Charley for eating it or at me for telling her to do it?"

"I'm mad at both of you," Myles said.
"But I guess I'm madder at you since you told her to do it."

His daddy smiled and winked at him, and Myles went upstairs to his room.

RUMBLE, YOUNG MAN, RUMBLE!

He was mad at Charley for eating the donut but she had to obey their daddy... just like Malcom had to obey their teacher.

"Oh no," Myles whispered. He felt bad. He had been mean to his best friend over something that wasn't his fault.

The next morning, Myles got to school early. He slid a note into Malcom's cubby that read "The clubhouse needs a hall monitor," and went to talk to Mr. Rasheed.

"Mr. Rasheed, could I please be
the hall monitor next week?"

Mr. Rasheed thought for a moment. "If you do a good job the rest of the week being the line leader, then the job is yours."

Myles thanked him and went back to the cubbies. By that time, Malcom was putting up his backpack.

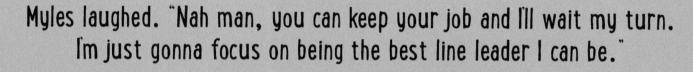

Myles laughed. "Nah man, you can keep your job and I'll wait my turn. I'm just gonna focus on being the best line leader I can be."

"Good!" Malcom said. "If you'll do your job, mine will be easier. You were the only person I had to get onto in the hall yesterday so pay attention today!"

The boys laughed and gave each other a pound. M&M were back!

CPSIA information can be obtained
at www.ICGtesting.com
Printed in the USA
BVHW090915171121
621700BV00003B/38